Jazz and Jeff

Written by Catherine Baker

Illustrated by Leo Brown

Collins

Jazz and Jeff sit and fish.

Thunk!

3

They hop in.

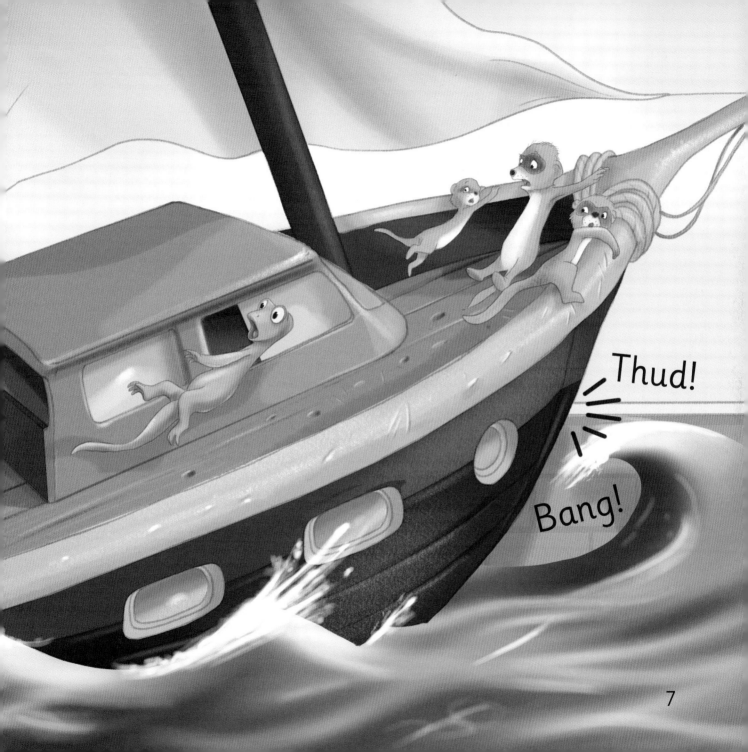

7

The ship zigzags.

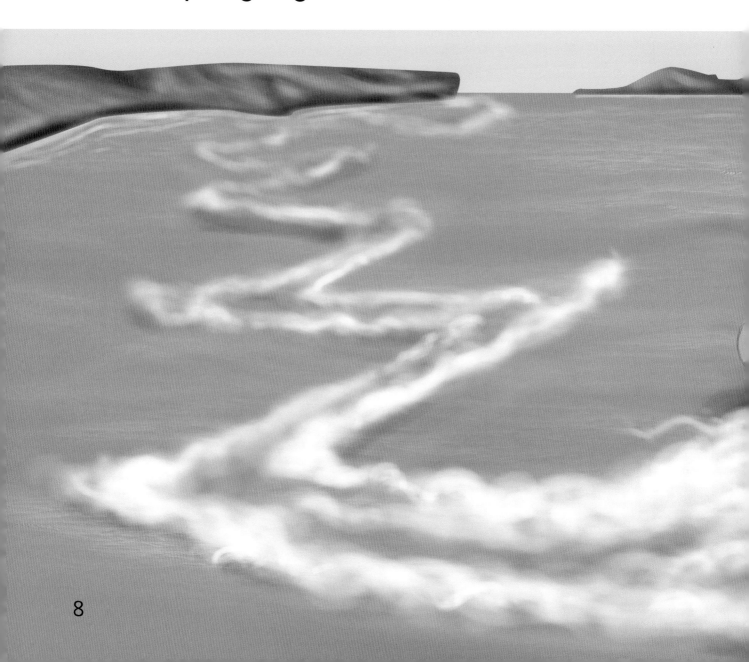

9

The ship sinks.

They tug the ship!

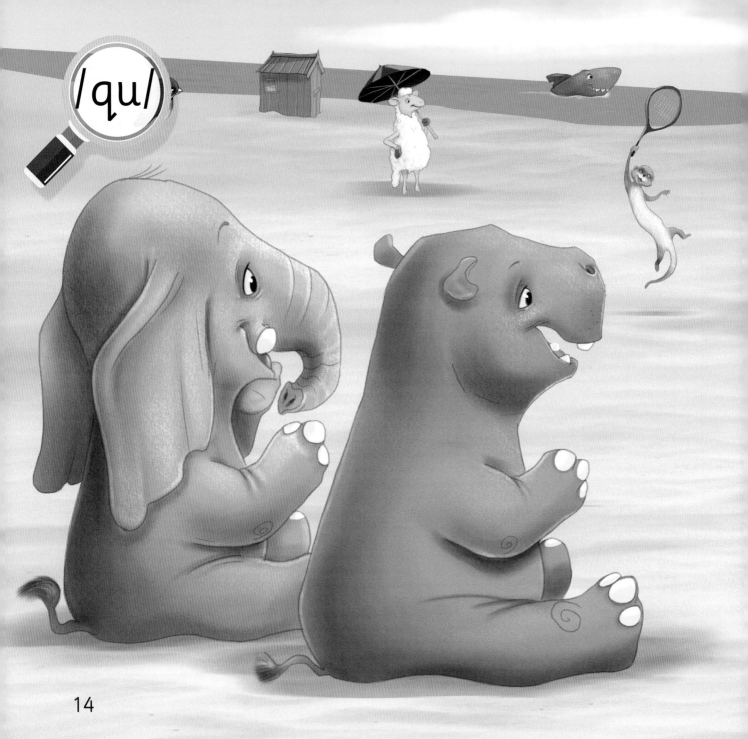

/qu/

14

/sh/

15

After reading

Letters and Sounds: Phase 3

Word count: 40

Focus phonemes: /z/ zz /th/ /sh/ /qu/ /ng/ /nk/ /x/ /w/ /j/

Common exception words: and, we, they, the

Curriculum links: Understanding the world

Early learning goals: Reading: read and understand simple sentences; use phonic knowledge to decode regular words and read them aloud accurately; read some common irregular words

Developing fluency

- Your child may enjoy hearing you read the book.
- Ask your child to read the sound labels and speech bubbles with expression, using a different tone for Jazz, Jeff and the meerkats.

Phonic practice

- Read pages 2 and 3. Ask your child to point to the two letters that make one sound in **Jazz**, **Jeff**, **fish** and **Thunk**. (*J/a/zz, J/e/ff, f/i/sh, th/u/nk*)
- Ask your child to sound out and blend the following:

  qu/i/ck   th/u/d   b/a/ng   r/u/sh   s/i/nk/s

- Look at the "I spy sounds" pages (14–15) together. Take turns to find a word in the picture containing a /qu/ or /sh/ sound. (e.g. *quick, quilt, queen*; *fish, ship, shuttlecock, shark, shed, sheep, shorts, shirt*)

Extending vocabulary

- Ask your child to suggest words or phrases with a similar meaning to these:

  hop on (page 4)   zigzags (page 8)   fix (page 11)   quick (page 13)